DATE DUE	
Hope	2018

We're Having A Tuesday

By DK Simoneau

Illustrated by Brad Cornelius

AC Publications Group LLC

Text copyright © 2006 by DK Simoneau
Illustrations copyright © 2006 by AC Publications Group LLC

Request for permission to make copies of any part of
the work should be mailed to the following address:
AC Publications Group LLC, Attention Permissions Department,
P.O. Box 260543 Lakewood, CO 80226

www.acpublicationsgroup.com

Book design & layout by Cherished Solutions, llc

Printed in Canada

First Edition   10 9 8 7 6 5 4 3 2 1

ISBN 9781933302133

Library of Congress Control Number: 2005904863

Type set in Cantoria MT. The art was prepared using Windsor Newton watercolors
and Berol colored pencils, on stretched 140 lb. Arches hot press paper.

"Fred, You have been my rock. xxoo, dk"

To Aurora and Carrington
...and all of our Tuesdays that I so
happily anticipate.

-D. K. S.

To Melissa, for her unfailing
support and limitless love.

-B.C.

It's Tuesday.

I slam the car door when I get home from school.
"I don't want to carry my jacket inside!"
I rip my brother's picture in half. "It's ugly anyway!"

I hear Mommy groaning,
"Are we having a Tuesday????"

I poke him in the arm
just to see if he'll get mad.

"Don't tattle!"

"Don't copy me!"

I just want to cover
up my ears and shout!

"Yes, it's Tuesday!
Go away!
Just leave me alone!"

My mommy and daddy are divorced,
so I don't live in just one house.

I've been at Daddy's
for the last three days.

I always come back to
Mommy's on Tuesday.

I can't wait to run and hug Mommy
because I'm so happy to see her.

I leap into her arms with
a big smile and kiss!

But then it starts.

"I wish I had my sneakers so I could go outside and ride my bike, but they're at Daddy's."

"My favorite skates aren't here, either."

"I really wish I could give my favorite teddy bear a great big hug, but I left her on my other bed!"

"But, Mommy, I really wanted to wear my favorite blue dress tomorrow!"

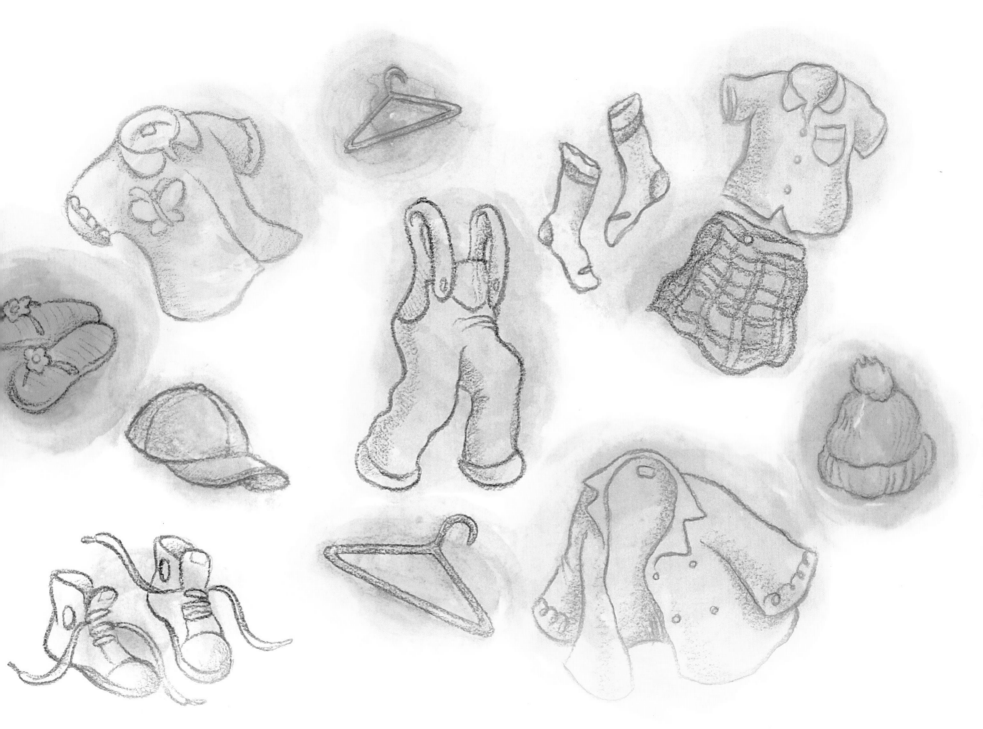

I even miss my clothes sometimes.

But most of all, I start feeling sad because I won't see Daddy again until Saturday. I miss him already.

I miss him making me giggle. I miss walking the dogs with him.

I miss my daddy tucking me in at night.

"Goodnight, princess!"

I miss him waking me with a backrub in the morning. "Time to wake up, sleepyhead!"

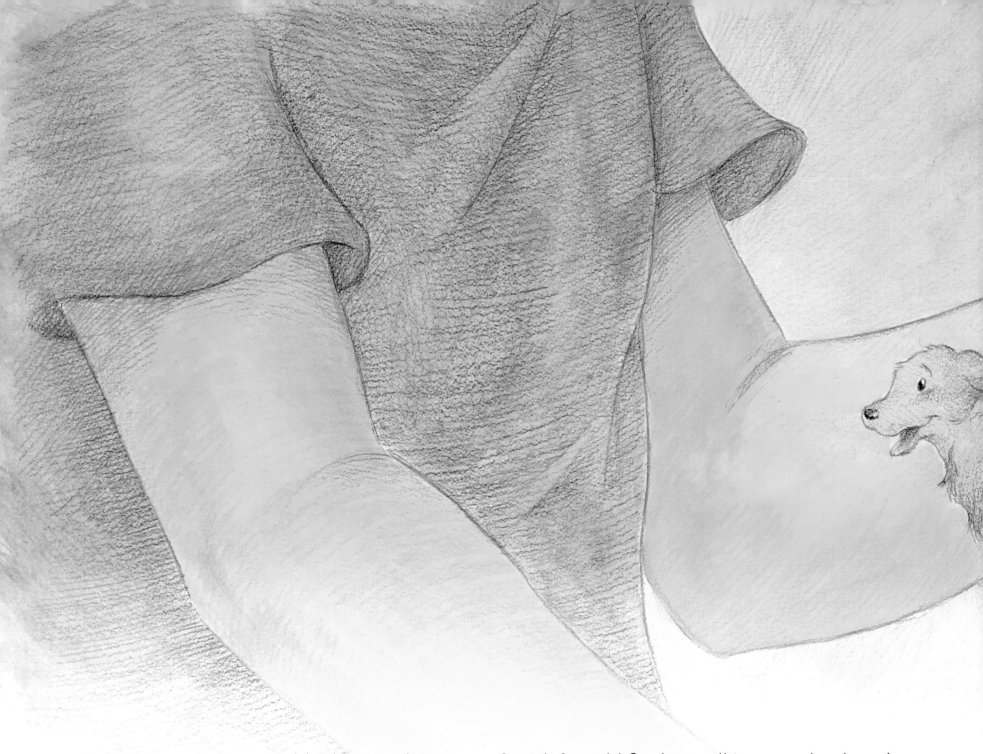

I miss my room, my blankets and my toys. I wish I could fit them all into my backpack.

I wish I could fit Daddy into my backpack, too!

I'll be at Mommy's for four days now. I know when I go back to Daddy's on Saturday, I'll miss Mommy, too. I'll miss running silly races with Mommy. I'll even miss her funny little songs and the way she cooks us good things to eat!

"Do you smell that?" I ask my little brother.

"Mmmm! That smells like something yummy! Like maybe bacon!"

I sneak around the corner
to the kitchen. I spot
Mommy cooking my favorite.

"Yeah! Breakfast for dinner! Eggs,
bacon, and waffles! I'll get the syrup!"

"Can we eat in
our favorite place?"
Mommy grins and nods yes.

I dash up to my room and grab my favorite little quilt that Mommy made especially for me.

I lay it out on the living room floor. My brother and I zoom back to our rooms to snatch all of our special fuzzy stuffed animal friends.

Then we plop them onto the living room floor, too!

"Thank you for living room picnics, little quilts, homemade waffles, and for Mommy!" We always say thank-yous before we eat at Mommy's.

Now I remember all of the things I wish I could pack into my backpack on Saturday when I go back to Daddy's...like waffles!

I wish I could pack my little patch quilt, my big fluffy bed, and even my warm fuzzy pajamas.

I'd tuck away Mommy's soft voice reading my favorite bedtime story.

I'd squeeze in my dolly with the tiny pink slippers, my little rocking chair, and my big bouncing ball….

But most of all, I wish I could zip in Mommy and her warm hugs and kisses right on top!

Sometimes I forget for a little while, but then I remember that no matter where I am, or who I am with, Mommy and Daddy are always tucked away in a very special kind of backpack.

They're in my heart.

"Mommy, after dinner can we put on our dance clothes and turn on the special lights and have a dance party?"

"Will you play our favorite songs and teach us to dance like you do?"

Yep, we're having a Tuesday, and I'm really glad!

Things I Miss About Mommy

Ways I can remember her

Things I Miss About Daddy

Ways I can remember him

More ways I can remember Mommy

More ways I can remember Daddy

The things Mommy remembers about me

The things Daddy remembers about me

author

Photo: Walter Freeman

DK Simoneau is a real-life divorced mother of two. Originally an accountant by profession, her children's love for books has inspired her to write stories that teach and validate as well as stimulate an everlasting curiosity in reading. She lives in Lakewood, Colorado, where she is currently working on several other book projects.

illustrator

Brad Cornelius has been drawing on restaurant napkins since he could hold a pen. As a grown-up, his illustrations have appeared in magazines, newspapers, school textbooks and catalogs. Children's books, however, have always been Brad's true passion. He currently resides in Evanston, Illinois, and this is his first book.